Be

Friends

PEANUTS WISDOM TO CARRY YOU THROUGH

Copyright © 2013 by Peanuts Worldwide LLC
Published by Running Press,
A Member of the Perseus Books Group
All rights reserved under the Pan-American and
International Copyright Conventions

Printed in China

Books published by Running Press are available at special discounts for bulk
purchases in the United States by corporations, institutions, and other organizations.
For more information, please contact the Special Markets Department at the
Perseus Books Group, 2300 Chestnut Street, Suite 200, Philadelphia, PA 19103, or
call (800) 810-4145, ext. 5000, or e-mail special.markets@perseusbooks.com.

ISBN 978-0-7624-5044-2
Library of Congress Control Number: 2013940509

9 8 7 6 5 4 3 2 1
Digit on the right indicates the number of this printing

Artwork created by Charles M. Schulz
For Charles M. Schulz Creative Associates: pencils by Vicki Scott,
inks by Paige Braddock, colors by Donna Almendrala
Designed by Frances J Soo Ping Chow
Edited by Marlo Scrimizzi
Typography: Archer, Clarendon, Futura, Gill Sans, Hypatia Sans Pro, Lobster Two,
Mission Script, and Memphis

Running Press Book Publishers
2300 Chestnut Street
Philadelphia, PA 19103-4371

Visit us on the web!
www.runningpress.com
www.snoopy.com

Be
Friends

PEANUTS WISDOM TO CARRY YOU THROUGH

Based on the comic strip, PEANUTS,
by Charles M. Schulz

RUNNING PRESS
PHILADELPHIA · LONDON

"Just thinking about a friend makes you want to do a happy dance, because a friend is someone who loves you in spite of your faults."

—*Charles M. Schulz*

Be
POLITE

"Yes, it does make you look taller."

—*Snoopy*

Be

CONTENT

"The secret of life is hanging around people who don't know the difference! Or whatever...."

—*Linus*

Be
a Cheerleader

"Come on, Charlie Brown. Strike this guy out! You can do it! We believe in you! I've always believed in you.... Hypocrite that I am."

—*Lucy*

Be HONEST

Peppermint Patty: The worst player always plays right field, and you're our worst player. But you wear your glove well, Marcie.

Marcie: Thank you, sir. I appreciate the compliment.

Be

Amazed

"You're the only one I know who can land
with backspin."

—*Snoopy*

HUMBLED

Charlie Brown: I feel good mentally, and I feel good physically. This is the most confident I've ever felt.

Sally: You've got grape jelly on your shirt.

Be
Accepting

Linus: Dogs accept people for what they are.

Snoopy: Oh?

Be

HELPFUL

Be

Loving

Be
FRANK

"When a person gets a new hairdo, you're supposed to tell her how nice it looks. You're not supposed to say, 'What happened to your head?'"

—*Peppermint Patty*

Be
SUPPORTIVE

"Joe Forklift."

—*Snoopy*

Be
LOYAL

Charlie Brown: What if you were the master and I was your dog?

Snoopy: I thought I was the master.

Be

Reliable

Sally: I'm doing a report for school on "Our Animal Friends." Can you give me any advice?

Snoopy: Sure, don't mention my name!

Be

Affectionate

"Happiness is a warm puppy."

—*Lucy*

Be

COMFORTING

"Owning a dog is a big responsibility, Rerun. They need lots of care. And they need a lot of comforting."

—*Charlie Brown*

Be
PROTECTIVE

Be

Appreciative

"The friendship of a boy and his dog is a beautiful thing. It touches me deeply to know that we mean more to each other than anything in the world."

—*Charlie Brown*

Be
COURAGEOUS

"Hang on! This is going to be the most exciting
ride of your life!"

—*Linus*

SYMPATHETIC

Charlie Brown: Why should a person be burdened with all the cares of the world?

Snoopy: Try sleeping.

Be
Nurturing

"I don't recall saying that you could share
this blanket."

—*Linus*

Be
SELFLESS

Be

Encouraging

"Just because you're small, you don't have to be afraid."

—*Snoopy*

Be

Playful

Be
INSPIRED

"I like the way you stand tall, and the way you seem to be reaching for the heavens. It's very inspiring."

—*Spike*

Be
EXCITED

"Every day when I come home from school,
he acts this way. He's so glad to see me!"

—*Charlie Brown*

Be
THANKFUL

"It's good to have a friend. Although I can see where having too many friends can be hard on the stomach!"

—*Snoopy*

Be
AGREEABLE

Be
Relaxed

Be
THERE

Linus: What's the cure for disillusionment, Charlie Brown?

Charlie Brown: A chocolate-cream and a friendly pat on the back.

Be
FULFILLED

Charlie Brown: A friendship like ours is worth all the money in the world.

Snoopy: On the other hand, if we had a little money we could buy some more cookies.

Lucy: A judge recently declared that a hockey stick is a "dangerous weapon." Do you agree?

Franklin: In all my years of playing baseball, I've never been hit with a hockey stick!

Be

TRUSTWORTHY

"So here I am left alone in the car again . . . , and with two sacks full of Chinese food in the back seat! They know I can be trusted though. . . . Except I opened all the fortune cookies."

—Snoopy

"I wish for a long life for all my friends."
—*Linus*

Be
NEAR

"We'll just sit here together until your mom flies by, and then you can give her the flower."

—*Snoopy*